NOBODY

NOBODY'S DOG

Eleanor Watkins

Dernier Publishing

London

Text Copyright © Eleanor Watkins
Illustrations by Josh Williams
Nobody's Dog was first published by Scripture Union in 1995.
The text has been updated.
This edition copyright © Dernier Publishing 2020

Published by Dernier Publishing
P.O. Box 793, Orpington, BR6 1FA, England
www.dernierpublishing.com

ISBN: 978-1-912457-42-7

Contents

1

The Dog in the Park

"There's that dog again," said Luke.

"Are you sure it's the same one?" asked Mum.

"Yes," said Luke. "I can tell by its tail. It's got a bushy tail like a fox, with a bit of white at the very end."

Mum came over to the window and looked down at the park with Luke. Spring was almost here, and the trees had fresh buds all ready to burst out.

There were the first yellow daffodils nodding their heads in the flower beds. But it was still cold outside, and people walked along with their coats on and heads down against the chilly wind.

Lots of dogs were being walked, because it was Sunday afternoon. Some were on leads and some were off, chasing balls or sticks or just running.

But this dog was all on its own. It was a medium size dog with a feathery tail and floppy ears. It had a brown and white coat and would have been quite pretty if it wasn't so thin. It stood on the grass near the laurel bushes, watching the people passing but keeping a good distance from them.

"It's a stray dog," said Luke. "It doesn't belong to anyone."

"Oh, I'm sure it must do," said Mum. "It's just wandered off, that's all. There aren't any stray dogs in the park. Or if there are, the Dog Wardens will soon round them up."

"What will they do with them?" asked Luke.

"They put them into kennels," said Mum. "If their owners don't come, they'll try to find a good home for them."

"But what if nobody wants them?" asked Luke.

"Well," Mum looked uncomfortable. Then she said, "Luke, your action figures are all over the table, and I want to set it for tea. Come and clear them all away."

Luke came and began to gather his toys together. He knew Mum didn't want to tell him what happened to unwanted dogs. That meant it must be something nasty.

He didn't like the thought of something nasty happening to the brown and white dog. He had seen it several times during the winter, from the window. Once or twice on his way to school he had seen it through the park railings. It looked lonely and sad, but he saw that it always kept well away from people and other dogs.

Pets were not allowed in the apartment block where Luke and his mother lived, except for little ones in cages, like budgies or hamsters.

Luke had a hamster himself, round and brown, which picked up food in its little paws and stuffed it into its cheeks until they were full. Then it spat all the food out into a store it had made at the back of the cage.

Luke was very fond of Hammy, but there wasn't a lot they could do together.

Luke liked living on the third floor of their apartment block, though Mum did not. She had put their names down for rehousing. She wanted somewhere with a garden, and hoped it would be soon. But Luke liked being able to see out over the road and into the park. He liked travelling up and down in the escalator, and even climbing the stairs when the escalators weren't working. He didn't mind not having a garden. But he did wish they were allowed to keep cats and dogs.

Luke and Mum had their tea and then they went to church as usual. Luke kept a look out for the brown and white dog as they passed the park. But the dog wasn't about.

After church, he asked Mum if they could go into the park for a while. Mum said they could, as the evenings were getting lighter now, and they were well wrapped up.

"But stay where I can see you," she said.

There were still people about in the park. The ice cream van and hot dog stand were beginning to pack up for the day. Daffodils were bright yellow against the grass, and tulips were showing their first bits of red. Luke ran round the circular flower bed keeping a look-out for the stray dog. Mum turned up her coat collar and sat down to rest on a bench.

There were still some dogs about, but all of them were with somebody. Luke hoped that the Dog Warden hadn't come and taken him away.

Then, suddenly, he saw the dog. It was standing quite near, at the edge of a clump of bushes, watching him but ready to run at any moment. Its ears were down and its tail between its legs, as though it expected to be chased away. Luke saw that its ribs showed under its brown and white coat. It was hungry.

"Hello, dog," said Luke softly.

The dog just stood and watched him. Then, suddenly, it turned and dived into the bushes. It disappeared among the dark green glossy leaves, but next moment Luke saw it come out at the back of the bushes. Then it ran off out of sight behind the shelters.

Luke parted the leaves and went a little way into the bushes, peering about in the dark green gloom. There, deep in the bushes, was a kind of scooped-out hollow in the ground. The leaves and twigs around it made a sheltered, secret hiding-place. This must be where the stray dog lived, with an escape exit at the back.

"Luke!" called Mum. "What are you doing? Come back over here, please."

Luke let the leaves fall back and ran over to Mum. He remembered the dog's hungry brown eyes and the way its ribs stuck out. "Mum," he said, "could I have a hot dog?"

Mum looked doubtfully across to the hot dog stand. "I think the man's packed up for the night."

"Not quite," said Luke. "If I'm quick."

The man served him a lukewarm hot dog with the last scrapings of fried onions.

Luke ran over and pushed it through the leaves, putting it on the ground just in front of the scooped-out hollow.

"Whatever are you doing?" asked Mum.

"It's for Bushy," said Luke.

"Who on earth is Bushy?"

"The dog," said Luke. "The stray dog. I think he lives in those bushes. And he's got a bushy tail. I thought Bushy would be a good name for him."

"Oh, Luke," said Mum. "It was kind of you, but don't ever try to touch that dog, will you? Especially if there's food about. Dogs like that can be dangerous."

"Bushy's not dangerous," said Luke. "Just lonely and sad."

"Well, all the same," said Mum, "remember what I've told you. That dog will probably be taken away soon. Dogs like that just aren't allowed to run wild here, and a good thing too. Just forget about him. Come on, it's cold and it's getting dark."

Luke followed her, putting his cold hands into his jacket pockets. But he knew he would not forget the brown and white dog.

2

Mr Bronzovi

The days were growing longer and warmer and spring was really here. Birds were singing, and tulips were bright red in the park beds. Luke noticed the brown and white dog more and more. Almost always he was in the park, though once or twice he saw him running along the pavement and squeezing through the park railings.

"I just can't understand how he gets away with it," said Mum one day, as she and Luke watched the dog sniffing about in the park. Why hasn't he been caught? Where does he live? What on earth does he eat?"

Luke thought he knew the answers to all those questions. Bushy had not been caught because he was much too clever. He knew how to tell when the dog-catcher people were about and to run and hide from them. And Luke was sure that he lived in the secret little den in the bushes.

As for food, he had watched the dog eat many different things. Ends of sandwiches left by picnickers, or the remains of takeaways and burgers which people often dropped in the streets on Saturday nights. Then there were the back doors of restaurants like the one just down the road. One evening, Luke had watched Bushy trotting home from there with a large bone in his mouth. Bushy knew where to find things to eat, all right, even if he didn't always get enough.

Luke didn't say any of these things. Instead, he asked, "Mum, if the rules were changed about pets, could we have Bushy for our dog?"

Mum hesitated, seeing the pleading look on Luke's face. Mum had been brought up in the countryside with lots of sheep and chickens and ducks and cats and dogs. That was why she wanted a place with a garden, so that Luke could grow up with animals and growing things, the way she had.

She sighed, and said, "Well, maybe if the rules were changed. He might just be lost. He might already have a nice owner somewhere."

Luke knew Bushy didn't have a nice owner somewhere, or he'd have gone home instead of to the park.

"And he'd have to be wormed and treated for fleas and inoculated," his mum continued.

"What's inoculated?" asked Luke.

"It means an injection to protect dogs from diseases they can get."

"And then could he be our dog?"

Luke could see that Mum was still not keen on the idea.

She said, "A nice puppy would be better than a stray. But I'm afraid it's not going to happen, Luke. The rules won't be changed."

"They might," said Luke. "If I pray to God very hard about it. God is more important than the people who make the rules, isn't he?"

He did pray, every night, just after he had taken his last look at the park from the bedroom window.

* * * * *

At Easter, Mum got a part-time evening job as a waitress in a pizza place. She said the extra money would mean they could have a holiday in the summer. Some evenings, Luke went round to his friend Paul's house while Mum worked. Other times, he stayed with old Mr Bronzovi, who lived in the basement apartment downstairs. Mr Bronzovi and his wife had been very kind to Luke and his mum when they first moved to the apartments. After Mrs Bronzovi died, Mum and Luke spent as much time as they could with Mr Bronzovi, because he was lonely.

Luke liked staying with Mr Bronzovi, better than going anywhere else. Luke's father had been gone since Luke was a baby, and Luke hardly remembered him. Both his grandfathers lived hundreds of miles away, but Luke thought Mr Bronzovi made up for all this.

Mr Bronzovi was Polish, and in English his name meant Mr Brown. He had been in almost every country in the world when he was younger, and had collected interesting things from everywhere he went.

He had things made of wood from Africa and India and things made of brass and copper from the Middle East. There was an interesting story to tell about each one.

Mr Bronzovi and Luke sometimes crossed the road and went to the park now that the evenings were fine and warm. Luke was allowed to take his football, and play on the swings and slides, as long as he kept in sight of the park bench where Mr Bronzovi sat. If any of his friends were there Luke went to play with them, but he liked it just as much when he and Mr Bronzovi just sat and talked on the bench.

One evening, as they sat there, Bushy came sniffing along one of the paths, looking for any stray crisps or sandwich crusts that might be about.

"There's that young dog again," said Mr Bronzovi.

"Bushy," said Luke. "That's his name. I thought of it."

He wondered whether to tell Mr Bronzovi about the den in the bushes, but decided not to, for the moment anyway.

Mr Bronzovi nodded two or three times. "Bushy. I like that."

Someone had dropped part of a sausage from the hot dog stall. They watched the dog find it and gobble it down. Luke rummaged in his pocket and found a few crisps left in a packet. He jumped down and tipped them out on the grass. Bushy put his tail between his legs and darted away, with a frightened glance over his shoulder. He didn't go far, just around behind the bushes, but he wouldn't come and eat Luke's crisps.

Luke was disappointed. "I'm sure he's hungry."

The old man nodded again. He had white hair, cut very short, and a white beard. His eyes were very blue and he wore a blue cap with a peak in front. "Yes. But he won't take food from you. Nor from anyone else. I've watched him. He'll scrounge here and there and raid the bins. He'll clear up bits from the grass, when everyone has gone. But he won't take anything from a human soul. He keeps himself well away from everybody. It's a miracle he hasn't been caught before now."

Mr Bronzovi shook his head. "Someone's ill-treated him, sometime or another. That's what I think. He can't trust anyone, you see, not any more."

"I wouldn't hurt him," said Luke. "And you wouldn't either, would you? He could trust us."

"Tak," said Mr Bronzovi, which Luke knew meant "yes" in Polish. "But he doesn't know that. He thinks all people are the same."

Luke stopped swinging his legs and thought for a moment. Then he said, "Couldn't we get him to trust us?"

Mr Bronzovi thought, too. "Maybe. If he saw us often enough and got used to us. Maybe then."

"If he trusted us, Mum might let us keep him," said Luke wistfully. "If he went to the vet first. If God changed the rules about no pets."

"It isn't God who makes those sort of rules," said Mr Bronzovi. "It's the people in those official places who do that."

"But God is more important than them," said Luke. "Isn't he? And he knows all about Bushy, doesn't he?"

Mr Bronzovi nodded several times. "Tak. You can be sure he knows all about our Bushy."

"Then I'll keep on asking him," said Luke. Suddenly he had a new idea. "Mr Bronzovi, if we brought Bushy something he really likes, then he might believe we like him. Wouldn't he? Something like ice cream?"

Mr Bronzovi thought again, and for such a long time that Luke wondered whether he had dropped off to sleep.

Then the old man thumped his fist on his knee quite suddenly, and said, "Tripe!"

Luke jumped. "What, Mr Bronzovi?"

"Tripe. That's what dogs like. Green tripe! I'll get some from the butcher's tomorrow, nice and fresh. We'll try him with that. See if that works."

Luke swung his legs again, suddenly feeling very happy.

"That's a really good idea, Mr Bronzovi. Could you wait till I get home from school, do you think? Then Bushy will think the green tripe is from me as well."

3

Making Friends

Mr Bronzovi brought the tripe home next day in a plastic bag. Luke went to look at it when he came home from school. It looked disgusting and smelled even worse. Luke held his nose. But Mr Bronzovi looked pleased, and said it was just the sort of good stuff no dog could resist. He said he'd seen a lot of dogs in his time, and he'd never known one which turned up its nose at green tripe.

Luke wanted to go to the park with Mr Bronzovi, but Mum said no. She said that if Mr Bronzovi wanted to feed the stray dog, that was his business. She did not want Luke getting mixed up with it. She did not really trust Bushy, and you never knew what might happen.

Luke thought that for someone who had grown up with lots of animals, Mum could be a very worrying kind of person. But it was no use arguing with her once she had made up her mind. He had to be content with watching Mr Bronzovi from the windows of the apartment.

Later he saw Mr Bronzovi cross the road to the park, wearing his blue peaked cap and carrying the plastic bag.

A couple of other dogs on leads stopped and sniffed the air when Mr Bronzovi went by. Mr Bronzovi turned and waved to Luke with his free hand, and stuck up his thumb. Then he went into the park and sat on the seat just inside.

It was not long before Bushy appeared, edging along just by the bushes and keeping a look-out for people and other dogs. Mr Bronzovi got up carefully, took the plastic bag and seemed to be testing the wind to see which direction it was coming from. Then he spread some of the tripe on the ground so that the smell of it would blow towards Bushy, and went to sit down again.

Luke saw Bushy stop and put his nose in the air, sniffing. He sniffed for a long time, turning his head this way and that. He looked longingly towards the pile of tripe and licked his lips with a long pink tongue. He began to pace back and forth, moving in a wide semi-circle, but never coming any nearer to the tripe. All the time, he kept his eyes on Mr Bronzovi, ready to run at any moment.

Luke punched the air with his fists. "Oh, go on, Bushy, go on! Eat it! Mr Bronzovi's your friend!"

Mr Bronzovi sat waiting on the bench for a very long time. Luke watched at the window all that time too. And all the time, Bushy paced up and down, sniffing the air, or sat down with his ears cocked, ready to run at the least alarm. Nothing would persuade him to come near Mr Bronzovi, not even the best green tripe.

In the end, Mr Bronzovi got up stiffly. He looked up at Luke in the window, spread out his hands and shrugged his shoulders. Bushy leapt to his feet and darted off nervously round the bushes as soon as Mr Bronzovi moved. The old man gathered up the plastic bag and began to shuffle towards the park gate, looking dejected.

"Mr Bronzovi!" shouted Luke suddenly.

Mr Bronzovi couldn't hear at that distance, but he happened to glance up at Luke's window again just at that moment. Luke waved and pointed. As

Mr Bronzovi walked away, Bushy had crept out from the bushes and began to approach the tripe.

By the time the old man had reached the gate and turned, the dog was eagerly devouring his meal. Afterwards he licked his lips and looked towards the gate and the apartments, just for a moment. Luke was sure that he knew they'd brought the tripe – he and Mr Bronzovi. He and Mr Bronzovi put up their thumbs to one another. Mr Bronzovi stopped shuffling and walked home with quite a spring in his step.

* * * * *

For several days, Mr Bronzovi brought fresh tripe from the butcher's. It was smelly and horrid-looking, but delicious to a hungry stray dog like Bushy. He took it to the park every day, at the same time, and spread it out in the same place. Then he sat on the seat, while Luke watched from the window. Sometimes Bushy was about and sometimes he wasn't. But always, when Mr Bronzovi got up to go home, Bushy would appear and gobble down the meal.

Then Mr Bronzovi began bringing other food instead of tripe – meat scraps, sausage, whatever he had left over from his own dinner. Bushy did not seem to mind the change of menu. As soon as Mr Bronzovi left, he came out of hiding and ate up whatever was on offer. He now expected Mr Bronzovi to bring his supper every day.

* * * * *

One evening, things happened in a different way. Instead of waiting for Mr Bronzovi to walk away as usual, Bushy appeared from the bushes while the old man was still sitting on the seat. He sniffed the air, looked at Mr Bronzovi, sniffed again and then trotted across to the food the old man had brought. He ate it all up and licked his lips. Then he looked at Mr Bronzovi again and trotted away into the bushes, in no great hurry.

"He's beginning to trust me at last," Mr Bronzovi told Luke. Mum had left for work and Luke had gone to stay at the basement apartment. "I do believe he really is. And he's getting fatter, with proper regular meals. His ribs don't stick out any more."

He and Luke had a drink of fizzy lemonade to celebrate.

Mum had watched Bushy enough herself to see that he was not a dangerous dog, just a very shy one. Now she let Luke go to the park with Mr Bronzovi when Bushy was fed.

Mum was feeling cheerful because she had been told they might be rehoused sooner than expected. Luke hoped that the new house wouldn't be too far away. He wanted to stay near the park and Mr Bronzovi, especially now that Bushy was really beginning to trust the two of them.

4

Taking Care of Bushy

One evening, when Luke and Mr Bronzovi went to the park, Bushy wasn't there. They had brought the remains of a meat pie, with extra gravy, in a plastic container. They took off the lid and put the container on the grass, then sat down to wait.

But Bushy did not come. A few other dogs came and sniffed at the pie, and Mr Bronzovi shooed them away. They waited and waited, but there was no sign of Bushy.

Luke began to feel worried. "Do you think those dog-catcher people came?"

Mr Bronzovi shook his head. "I don't think so. I think we would have seen something. A van, or men. Something going on."

"Then where is he?"

Luke could see that Mr Bronzovi looked worried too. "I don't know. He never misses a day, usually. Let's take a walk and see what we can see."

There were lots of people in the park now that the warm evenings were here. Birds chirped and hopped about in the bushes. Down the path came another elderly man, a friend of Mr Bronzovi's. The two old men politely raised their caps to one another, and said good evening.

There was a lot of noise coming from near the sports pitches. A group of big boys were shouting and kicking a coke can about. Mr Bronzovi's friend tut-tutted. "Hooligans! Shouldn't be allowed! Terrible what they did to that poor dog this morning!"

Luke and Mr Bronzovi both stared at him. "What was that?" asked Mr Bronzovi. "What dog was that?"

"That dog that's always about. That stray one you've been feeding. Saw them when I went for my newspaper this morning. Chasing him with sticks and stones, they were. Wouldn't leave him be. I shouted at them but they only laughed."

"Where did he go?" asked Mr Bronzovi. "Did you see?"

The other old man shook his head. "Ran off, with them after him. Round the back of the shelters. Frightened half to death."

He went on down the path, shaking his head. Mr Bronzovi and Luke looked at each other. Mr Bronzovi's bushy white eyebrows were drawn together in a frown.

"Where do you think he went?" asked Luke in a small voice. But Mr Bronzovi could only shake his head.

Suddenly Luke remembered the secret den in the bushes.

He had never told anyone about it except Mum. Could Bushy be hiding there? He ran away across the grass to the bushes, leaving Mr Bronzovi behind.

Mr Bronzovi caught up with him, puffing and blowing. "You should not run off like that, young man. My old bones can't keep up."

"Sorry," said Luke. "Only I thought

of something. Bushy might be in here. This is his secret den." He parted the leaves and looked in.

A dark shape lay still in the scooped-out place. Darker patches of dried blood showed against a brown and white coat. Bushy's eyes were closed.

Luke felt his own eyes fill with tears. He let the leaves fall back. "He's dead, Mr Bronzovi. Bushy's dead. Those boys killed him with their sticks and stones."

"Here, let me look." Mr Bronzovi got down stiffly on his hands and knees and crawled in among the bushes. Luke could hear him muttering and grunting. Then he came out backwards and got to his feet.

"He's not dead. But he's in a bad way. Lost a lot of blood. And half-stunned. Frightened stiff, too. He would have run a mile from me if he hadn't been so weak."

"Oh, poor Bushy!" said Luke. "What shall we do?"

Mr Bronzovi thought for a moment, dusting the soil from his hands. "By rights we ought to tell the police. And the vet. But then they'd report him to the Dog Warden. They'd take him away and shut him up in a pen. I don't think he'd like that."

"He'd hate it," said Luke. "Can't we look after him ourselves? Just until he's well again?"

"I suppose we could try," said Mr Bronzovi. "Tak. We could try. We'll get some milk for him. With a drop of brandy. Only you mustn't go too close, or your mother will never trust me again."

They walked home and fetched warm milk in another plastic container. Mr Bronzovi crawled stiffly into the bushes with it. Luke followed, although he knew Mum would not like it. But he was sure Bushy would not bite, even if he was hurt and frightened.

Bushy didn't bite when Mr Bronzovi touched him gently. He didn't snap or even growl. But he did look very scared, and would have got up and run if he had not been so sick. He cowered away, and tried to press himself flatter against the ground.

"It's a shame," said Mr Bronzovi. "He was hurt before and now he's been hurt again. No wonder he can't trust people. He's been neglected. Come on, old friend. Drink this. It'll help you get strong again."

He talked gently and soothingly to the dog. Luke squatted down on the damp-smelling soil and watched. He saw that one of Bushy's eyes was swollen half-shut, and there was blood on his nose and side and leg.

But at last Mr Bronzovi managed to get the dog to raise his head and drink a few drops of milk.

"That will do for now," said Mr Bronzovi. "We'll leave him to rest and come again tomorrow."

Walking home along the path, Luke felt sad.

"Why did God let that happen, Mr Bronzovi? After we asked him to take care of Bushy?"

"Ach," said Mr Bronzovi, "who can tell? But I know this much. God is good. And he can turn things around, even the bad things that happen. He can make good come, even from something like this. We have to trust him."

* * * * *

Bushy lay in the bushes for several days. Two or three times a day, Mr Bronzovi took milk and water and tasty things across for him. Bushy began to get stronger. He sat up and licked his sore places. The bruises and cuts were healing up.

On the fourth evening, Bushy was on his feet again. Luke saw a brown nose peeping out of the bushes and two brown eyes watching.

"He's waiting for us," said Luke.

"So he is," said Mr Bronzovi. "Come on then, old friend. Here is your supper. Come and get it."

Slowly, Bushy's head came out of the bushes, and then the rest of him. He limped a little, but less than the day before. He stood for a moment, shook himself and then walked over to them. He looked at Mr Bronzovi and then at Luke, before he ate his supper. Then he looked at them again.

"He's saying thank you," said Luke.

"I do believe he is," said Mr Bronzovi. "He has good manners. He is a good dog." He reached out and touched Bushy, stroking his head and neck and ears. Then he scratched his back and sides. Bushy quivered but he didn't run. Then he stopped quivering and stood still as though he was enjoying the fuss. His tongue came out in a doggy smile. And then his long feathery tail began to wave slowly from side to side.

5

Disappointment

Every day now it got warmer and the
evenings were lighter. The park gardener
had dug up the flowering bulbs and
planted little marigolds and pansies in
their places. One day, Luke and Mr
Bronzovi clearly heard a cuckoo calling
among the tall beech trees in the park.

Mr Bronzovi said that meant summer was only just around the corner.

It seemed to Luke that Mr Bronzovi looked younger these days. He walked straighter, with a spring in his step.

Bushy's cuts and swellings and bruises had all healed up. Every evening he pranced to meet them, waving his feathery tail and grinning a big doggy smile. His eyes were bright and his ears cocked. When he had eaten, he would look around at them both and wag his tail again. Then he would let Mr Bronzovi pat his head and stroke his ears.

"He's a fine dog," said Mr Bronzovi. "The kind of dog anyone would be proud to own. I wish..."

"What, Mr Bronzovi?" asked Luke. "That he was your dog?"

The old man nodded his head in the blue peaked cap.

"Exactly. He doesn't wear a collar so that means he doesn't belong to anyone. He's nobody's dog. Every dog ought to have someone to belong to. If only we were allowed pets."

He sighed. Luke sighed, too. Every evening, when they left the park, Bushy stood looking sadly after them, with his head on one side, trying to understand why they were leaving him. If only they could take him home with them, the way other people did with their dogs.

"I wonder..." said Mr Bronzovi thoughtfully. Luke saw that his blue eyes were twinkling suddenly. "What, Mr Bronzovi?"

"I wonder. The rules say that residents must not have pets to live with them. They say nothing about having animals to visit. Would it hurt for Bushy to come in the daytime? As long as he didn't stay overnight?"

He and Luke looked at each other. Luke felt a little flicker of excitement.

They could take Bushy to Mr Bronzovi's basement apartment, feed him, brush him, even bath him. He could sit with them while they watched TV. He would save up and buy one of those comfy padded dog baskets for him.

He said eagerly, "Do you think he'd come?"

Mr Bronzovi put his hands on his knees and looked at Bushy, stretched out near them on the grass, dozing. "I think he would. Only we'd need a collar and lead, because of the road."

"Would they cost a lot?"

"New ones might. But I'll see. I'll ask around."

* * * * *

Next day Mr Bronzovi pulled a dog collar and lead from his overcoat pocket. "Not new, but as good as. Quite cheap, from the charity shop. And real leather."

He looked excited. Luke felt excited too. He couldn't wait to see what Bushy thought of the collar and lead.

They let Bushy eat his supper first, before they told him anything about it. Mr Bronzovi made a fuss of the dog, scratching his back and sides and telling him how good he was. Then he picked up the collar and lead from the bench.

Luke held his breath. Bushy quivered a little as Mr Bronzovi carefully fitted the collar round his neck, talking to him all the time. But his brown eyes looked trustingly up at the old man's, and he allowed him to fasten it snugly and clip on the lead.

Mr Bronzovi rewarded Bushy with another big fuss. "You're a good dog. The best in the world. That's what you are." He got creakily to his feet, holding the end of the lead. Bushy shook his head a little, as though the weight of the collar felt strange. Luke thought he looked a bit nervous. But when he felt the tug of the lead as Mr Bronzovi walked away, he trotted after him.

Mr Bronzovi saw that Luke felt like jumping about and waving his arms and shouting because he felt so happy. He put out a hand to stop him doing any of those things.

"Quietly now, quietly. All is going well and we don't want to startle him, do we? Let's take it easy."

"Are we going to take him home?"

"All in good time. First we get him used to walking with the lead."

They practised by walking round the flower beds and back to the seat. Mr Bronzovi said encouraging things to Bushy all the while. Then they thought they would try a longer walk to the shelters and back, before crossing the road.

All went well at first. Bushy trotted at heel as though he had been used to the lead all his life. Then, suddenly, things changed. Across the park came a man in a peaked cap and a white jacket. It was the park keeper, coming to empty the litter bins.

Suddenly, Bushy stopped. He began to tremble. Whether the man had shouted at him, or chased him, they did not know. Maybe it was just that he reminded Bushy of someone who had once hurt him. The man took no notice of them at all – an old man and a boy walking a dog on a fine evening in early summer.

"Come along, old friend," said Mr Bronzovi. "Everything is OK."

But suddenly, Bushy's eyes were wide

and frightened. He pulled away, jerking the lead from Mr Bronzovi's hands. Mr Bronzovi snatched at it but it was gone, bouncing over the grass as Bushy ran for cover. The end of it caught on a twig as he reached the bushes, but he pulled free and disappeared from sight.

Luke and Mr Bronzovi stared after him. "I was foolish," said Mr Bronzovi. "I wasn't careful enough."

Luke took his hand. "It wasn't your fault."

"I made a mistake," said Mr Bronzovi with a sigh, gazing across at the bushes where the dog had gone. "To think he would come with me."

"He nearly came," said Luke. "I think he wanted to."

Mr Bronzovi shook his head. "And

now he may get all tangled up with that lead. He may choke, all alone."

Luke felt alarmed. But he said, "I'm sure he won't, Mr Bronzovi. He's too sensible."

Mr Bronzovi's shoulders sagged. The spring had gone out of his step and he looked old again. "Ah well. Maybe you're right. Maybe he'll come back tomorrow and I can take it off him. It was a good collar and lead that, a good bargain. I'm a foolish old man, Luke. Tak. I'd better take you home to your mother."

6

Bushy Comes Home

The next day was Saturday, so there was no school. Luke usually watched cartoons on TV in the morning while Mum did housework, then they went out together in the afternoons. This morning, Luke was at the window, still thinking of Bushy and hoping he was not entangled with the lead somewhere in the bushes.

To his surprise, there was Mr Bronzovi crossing the road. Usually he didn't go out as early as this. Luke guessed that he, too, was worried about the dog.

Inside the park gates, Mr Bronzovi began to call Bushy's name, looking about in all directions.

Luke pressed his nose against the glass, watching. He didn't have long to wait. Almost at once, out of the bushes came trotting a brown and white dog, tail waving from side to side.

Luke could not tell whether he still had a collar, but there was no sign of a lead. Bushy hadn't got caught in the bushes and choked. And he still liked Mr

Bronzovi, because he went up to him at once, wanting to have a fuss made of him.

Mr Bronzovi stroked and patted Bushy and sat on the bench for a while with the dog at his feet. Luke kept one eye on them from the window seat, and the other eye on the TV cartoons. When Mr Bronzovi got up to come home, Luke thought that Bushy would go back to the bushes.

But he didn't. At first he stood watching as the old man made his way to the street gate.

"Mr Bronzovi!" shouted Luke suddenly.

Mr Bronzovi couldn't hear from that distance, and he couldn't see what Luke saw. As Mr Bronzovi began to cross the road, Bushy had trotted forward and was following close at his heels, all by himself.

"Mum!" shouted Luke. "I'm going down to Mr Bronzovi's, OK?"

By the time Mr Bronzovi arrived home, Luke was waiting in the lobby for him, breathless with excitement.

Mr Bronzovi had noticed the dog by that time and came in quietly, holding the door for Bushy to follow. He saw Luke and held his finger to his lips so that Luke would not startle him. But Bushy came in quite willingly, wagging his tail harder than ever as he recognised Luke. He followed them down the steps to Mr Bronzovi's apartment and looked up at them expectantly to see what they would do next.

"Welcome, my friend," said Mr Bronzovi softly. "Welcome home."

He found some cooked mince intended for his own dinner and gave it to Bushy on a tin plate. Bushy licked the plate clean, wagged his tail and lay down on the rug with his nose on his paws.

Luke and Mr Bronzovi looked at each other. It was as though Bushy had always lived here in the cosy, cluttered, basement apartment.

"What do we do now?" asked Luke.

"Flea powder," said Mr Bronzovi. "Worm tablets. Inoculations, when the vet's surgery is open. A bath."

"Can I help?"

"Whatever will your mother say?"

Luke wasn't sure about that. But, as it happened, Mum was quite happy to let him stay with Mr Bronzovi for the afternoon. Someone had phoned about her rehousing application and she was off out in a great hurry.

Luke half-listened during lunch as she was talking to him, but most of his mind was in the basement apartment. He mentioned that Bushy had followed Mr Bronzovi home, but knew that she was only half-listening too.

They left Bushy dozing indoors while they went along to the shops for flea powder and worming tablets. The spring had come back to Mr Bronzovi's step.

"I worried half the night about that

dog," he told Luke. "Then I remembered to pray. God has surely answered."

"What happened to the collar and lead, do you think?" asked Luke.

"Ach. Who can tell? I think he worked at it until it came off over his head. Anyway, what does it matter? A worn-out old lead from a charity shop! He deserves better, our dog. Tak."

"Tak," agreed Luke, although he knew that Mr Bronzovi was only trying to make him feel better. He remembered what Mr Bronzovi had said about everything working out for good, even the bad things. Then he remembered his own prayers. He was going to ask if Mr Bronzovi thought the rules about pets would be changed soon. But they had reached the chemist's and were going in.

When they got back to the apartment they were surprised by a big, deep "Woof!" as they opened the door. Bushy was in the hallway. But he stopped barking and his tail waved in welcome when he saw who it was.

"A good house-dog too!" said Mr Bronzovi in delight. "What a treasure this dog is!"

Bushy swallowed the tablets but was suspicious of the flea powder.

Mr Bronzovi decided that they would use his own bath-tub to bath him. Bushy didn't like the idea of that at all, and hid behind a chair as soon as he heard the running water. He trembled and put his tail between his legs.

It took Mr Bronzovi and Luke together to coax him out and lift and heave him into the warm soapy water. To start with he sat shivering in misery while they were rubbing and soaping and rinsing him, looking up at them as if begging them to finish soon, but he soon got used to it.

The bath water was very dirty after Bushy's bath. They drained it away and rubbed him briskly with an old towel as he crouched in the empty bath-tub.

He looked much smaller than usual with his wet coat plastered close to his skin. As soon as he got the chance, he leapt from the bath and gave himself a good shake all over the mat, and all over Luke and Mr Bronzovi too.

They dried themselves off.

"He'll have a lovely coat when it's dry," said Mr Bronzovi proudly.

Luke thought so too, when Bushy was dry and his coat was shiny and soft with the brown very bright and the white very clean. They brushed him with an old hairbrush. They could see that he felt better too, and soon forgot how horrid the bathing had been.

But the awful thought nagged at Luke that Bushy would have to go back to the park later and stay there for the night, all alone. He just wouldn't understand. He would think they were deserting him.

Mum called for him while Bushy was still there so he didn't see what happened after all. She was quite cross when she learnt how they had spent the afternoon.

"Taking that dog into his apartment? Bathing him in his own bath-tub? Really, I expected better of Mr Bronzovi! I always felt I could absolutely trust him. Being friends with a stray dog out of doors is one thing, but bringing him in and handling him like that is quite another. The dog could have turned on you both. You might have been badly bitten."

"Bushy wouldn't bite," said Luke.

"You can never tell," said Mum darkly. "And I've never heard of anything so unhygienic as using your own tub to bath a stray dog! What about diseases? Infections?"

"We put flea powder on. And he's going to the vet soon. And I expect Mr Bronzovi will clean the bath before he gets in himself."

Mum wouldn't listen. She rushed around, getting changed and making Luke wash and change too.

"Why?" asked Luke.

"We're going out," said Mum. "A house has come up, over on the other side of the park, and we're going to see it."

7

The New House

They could have walked, but Mum was so eager to get to the house that they took the bus to the other side of the park. Looking back when they got off, they could see their own apartment block opposite, but it was too far to pick out their own windows.

The house stood back from the road in its own garden. It was built of brick, faded to a pinkish shade. One or two of the windows were broken and boarded up. Even Luke could see that the roof needed repairing.

But what struck him most was the garden itself. Long grass, starred with daisies and buttercups, covered the front lawn. A tangle of honeysuckle and pink roses gone wild, climbed all over the fence at the side. The house itself was partly covered with pink and white striped clematis that twined and trailed over the pinky-red walls. Tall flowering plants and weeds and nettles jostled each other in overgrown borders. There was a big old apple tree near the fence.

Luke tried to take in everything at once. "Mum," he said, "it's – it's like a special park all of our own!"

Mum's eyes were shining. "Yes, it is, isn't it? All our own! I knew you'd like it!" Then she seemed to pull herself together. "Of course, the house is in very bad repair. It hasn't been lived in for ages. That's why it's such a bargain. But it'll need an awful lot of work to do it up. Let's go and look indoors."

Inside, the house was damp and dusty and neglected. Paper hung in strips from walls, paint was peeling and tiles needed replacing. Their voices echoed in the emptiness.

"It's lonely," said Luke. "It needs somebody to live in it."

He ran upstairs, into each of the

three bedrooms and the bathroom. The branches of a pear tree brushed the window of the smallest bedroom. "My room," said Luke to himself.

He ran downstairs again, feet clattering on the bare boards. He saw that the living-room had a fireplace in it, quite a big one, where they could build a real fire on cold evenings.

The kitchen opened on to the back garden, where there were several plum trees and a tangle of gooseberry bushes and raspberry canes.

Mum was standing in the long grass under the plum trees, face turned up to the sun. "You could almost imagine you're in the countryside! I could grow vegetables. Make jam. I wonder if we'd be allowed to keep chickens for eggs? Maybe I could have a beehive!"

"I could have a rabbit," said Luke. "Couldn't I?" He felt giddy with the space and the sunshine and the scent of honeysuckle.

"Yes," said Mum with a giggle in her voice. "You could." She grabbed Luke's hands and they danced around in a circle as though they were both five years old. Then they both collapsed on the grass.

"Do you really like it?" asked Mum breathlessly. "Would you like to come and live here?"

Luke had always thought he liked living in the third-floor apartment, looking out over the park, and liked climbing the stairs or going up in the elevator to get to it. But now he knew that what he wanted most in the world was to live in this tatty, pinky-red house with the glorious wild garden.

It was only later, going home on the bus, that he remembered Mr Bronzovi and Bushy.

"The three of us are friends now," he said. "I'd miss them. How would they get along without me?"

Mum was still the tiniest bit cross with Mr Bronzovi.

"They'd have each other," she said. "Maybe they'll be able to come across the park to visit."

Mr Bronzovi said the same when Luke told him their news. "We'll be happy for you, going to a lovely place like that. We could perhaps come and visit. Maybe even walk there across the park. Eh, old friend?"

Bushy thumped his tail on the hearth-rug. He had been for his inoculations and his coat had been brushed. Already he and Mr Bronzovi had got into a routine of peaceful days at home, walks, and then supper in the park. Bushy always looked a little puzzled when he was left behind in the park for the night, but was very pleased to see the old man in the morning.

"It's a long way," said Luke.

"Ach! What's a little distance like that between friends?"

* * * * *

Suddenly, all their spare time was spent at the house. They could move in fairly soon, they had been told. In the meantime, Mum was working hard on the place. There were many things they could not do themselves, and proper tradesmen would have to come in for those jobs. But she did all she could, especially in the neglected garden. She and Luke went there right after school to spend the long, light evenings. Together they cut grass and trimmed shrubs and rooted out weeds and nettles and planted seeds.

They had picnics outside or in the echoing empty rooms, sitting on folding chairs they had taken on the bus.

They planned exactly how they would arrange each room. Already it was beginning to feel like home.

* * * * *

For several days Luke saw little of Bushy and Mr Bronzovi. Then on Saturday morning there seemed to be a flurry in the street outside. Something was going on down there. Luke pressed his nose hard against the window to try and see what was happening. A white van was parked at the front entrance.

"Mum!" shouted Luke suddenly.

Two men were crossing the road from the park, to where the van stood waiting with its back door open.

They had something walking between them, something that seemed to be reluctant to go and was pulling back. Luke could just see a glimpse of a brown and white coat, very bright and clean. Bushy was resisting every inch of the way, digging his paws in, pulling back, his tail between his legs.

Luke banged on the window. "Stop it! Stop it! Let him go! You're not to take him!"

But if the men heard they took no notice. As he watched, they bundled the dog into the back of the van, closed the door behind him and were soon driving away.

8

Two Patients

Mum was almost as fast as Luke getting
downstairs to Mr Bronzovi's apartment,
to tell him what had happened to Bushy.
He took a long time answering the door
to them. When he came at last, he was
grey-faced and had a blanket draped
around his shoulders.

"Mr Bronzovi!" said Mum. "You're ill! You should be in bed."

Luke could see that Mum wasn't cross any more, not even the tiniest bit. Mr Bronzovi tried to reply but had a bad bout of coughing. Mum made him sit down in his armchair, with his feet on a stool. Then she put the kettle on for a hot drink.

Luke sat by Mr Bronzovi to keep him company while Mum was busy. Mr Bronzovi's blue eyes were sad.

"You saw them take the dog?" he asked huskily.

Luke nodded. He felt his own eyes fill with tears. "Yes. Why did they take him? Where's he going?"

The old man shook his head. "Wherever it is they take stray dogs.

All my fault. I kept him overnight, you see. Didn't feel like going out last night. Touch of my bronchitis. I let him out this morning." He coughed again, and went on, "To tell the truth, I wanted his company too. He's a good old friend, good company. Of course, someone had to notice and report him. That's why those men came and picked him up from the park."

"Who?" said Luke fiercely. "Who reported him? I'll go and thump them!"

"No, no," said the old man. "That's not the way. They were quite right and I was wrong. You have to keep the rules. I was foolish."

Luke felt helpless. He should have known that Mr Bronzovi was ill. But he had been so busy at the new house that he hadn't seen him and Bushy for days. It was his fault, too, as well as Mr Bronzovi's. And now Bushy had been bundled into the Dog Warden's van and taken away.

He wanted to put his head down on the arm of the chair and cry. But that would only make Mr Bronzovi feel worse. Mum was coming with steaming mugs on a tray, hot soup and triangles of toast for Mr Bronzovi.

"You're very good to me, Elizabeth," he said humbly. "I don't deserve it."

"Nonsense!" said Mum briskly. "You've always been wonderful with Luke. Now it's our turn to take care of you. I'll go and phone the surgery for a prescription. Then I'll see what's in your fridge and we'll do some shopping for you."

"But you are so busy. What about your new house?"

"It can wait," said Mum. "It won't run away. First things first. Luke, go and fetch another couple of cushions to make Mr Bronzovi comfortable. Then you can help me change the sheets."

All morning they were busy, cleaning and tidying Mr Bronzovi's flat and shopping and cooking for him. He looked more cheerful and said he felt better already. But sometimes Luke caught him looking sad, and knew he was thinking of Bushy. He thought of Bushy himself, nearly all the time, but he didn't say much. At home that night, and in church next morning, he prayed very hard for Bushy, and for Mr Bronzovi.

* * * * *

In three days Mr Bronzovi was much better. His pink colour had come back and he only coughed now and then. That evening, Mum met Luke after school and they caught the bus to the new house. Luke thought it felt just like going home. While Mum planted out some lettuces in the beds she had dug, he ran around looking at everything. He noticed that a bird had built a nest in the tangled honeysuckle, though the babies were hatched and flown away now. He saw that a thrush had been using a big flat stone nearby to crack snail shells.

The first raspberries were beginning to show a tinge of red. Mum gave Luke a plastic bowl and told him to find some ripe ones.

"See if you can get enough for Mr Bronzovi to have for his supper."

The builders had been and fixed the leaky roof, and put new glass in the broken windows. Mum sat back on her heels and looked at the pinky-red house with its garlands of clematis. "I really think we could move in soon," she said.

Both of them were tired when they got off the bus at their stop. The sun was setting and throwing long shadows over the park grass. For a moment, Luke thought he saw a movement that might have been a brown and white dog. Then he remembered that Bushy was gone. But he looked again, and there was something, just by the bushes. He narrowed his eyes against the sun to see better.

"Mum," he said. "Can we go into the park for a bit?"

"Oh, Luke," said Mum. "We're both tired, it's late and there's school tomorrow."

"Please! Just for a minute!"

In the end Mum agreed. She sank down on the bench, yawned, and stretched her arms. Luke ran to the bushes.

Suddenly Bushy was there, tongue lolling, tail waving, prancing round and round him. Luke could hardly believe it. But it was Bushy all right, although he looked a bit thin again. He seemed to have been hurt a little too, and limped on one foreleg. But he was delighted to see Luke.

Luke hardly dared to believe that Bushy was really there. He wondered how he had escaped.

Mum had her eyes shut. Luke gave Bushy a quick hug and ran over to her.

"Mum! Bushy's here! He's back! Look!"

Mum's eyes flew open. Luke could see that at first she thought he was making up stories. But Bushy had followed Luke and was standing there grinning at her, waving his long feathery tail.

"It's really him," she said wonderingly. "And whatever have they done to the poor dear? Luke, won't Mr Bronzovi be pleased?"

Luke couldn't wait to tell him. But he was still a little bit worried. "Mum, won't they come looking for Bushy again? Will they try to take him away again?"

Mum got up, putting on her most determined look. "Not if I can help it! They've already badly mistreated the poor thing, it's quite clear to see. Of course, Mr Bronzovi mustn't keep him overnight any more. But we can carry on as we were before, bringing him to the park after supper. I'll help until Mr Bronzovi's stronger."

"Will you?"

"Of course. I like Bushy very much now I've got to know him. And I was a country girl myself, remember? I know all about looking after animals. He'll need special care for a while, I expect. And a bit of feeding up. He can come over to Mr Bronzovi's apartment in the daytime and I'll look after the two of them together. Two patients are no more trouble than one."

9

Moving In

No one came looking for Bushy. He and Mr Bronzovi went back to spending their days together, with Mum to look after them. Mum had made enquiries and learnt that a dog with a collar was not classed as a stray. "He can't have been microchipped, or the Dog

Wardens would have taken him home," she observed. So she bought a brand new collar for Bushy with his name on a metal disc, though he still didn't have a proper address.

Each evening, Mum and Luke took Bushy across the road to give him his supper and leave him in the park.

"The nights are warm," said Mr Bronzovi. "It's no hardship to him. None at all."

"What will happen when winter comes, though?" asked Luke.

"The Lord will provide," said Mr Bronzovi. "He always does."

In a day or two, both Mum's patients were on the mend. Within a week they were both out and about, as good as new. It was just as well, because Mum had been told they could move to the new house.

Moving day was exciting. A van came and loaded up their furniture and all their belongings. The empty apartment looked very bare and strange. Luke went to look at the park for the last time.

"Not really for the last time," said Mum. "We'll still look out over the park from the new house."

"But it'll look different," said Luke. "Kind of back to front."

Mum laughed. They went downstairs for the last time. As usual, the lift was out of order so, as usual, they walked. The van was waiting at the entrance for them to climb into the front.

Mr Bronzovi and Bushy were waiting to say goodbye. All of a sudden, Luke felt funny inside. He wouldn't be popping in and out of the basement apartment any more. He wouldn't be staying there while Mum went to work. He wouldn't be going out with Bushy and Mr Bronzovi. They would be across the park, a bus ride away. Not far, but far enough.

Too far. Luke felt his lip quiver. He went and hugged Bushy, burying his face in his brown and white coat. It smelt of dog shampoo. Mum didn't mind him doing this, now that Bushy had been treated for everything nasty that dogs could get. Mum had grown quite fond of Bushy herself.

Bushy's tail waved. Mr Bronzovi cleared his throat.

"You keep a good look-out for us, now. Some nice afternoon, we'll stroll across the park to pay you a visit, Bushy and me. Tak."

Luke gulped. "It's a long way."

"What's a quarter of a mile between friends?"

Mr Bronzovi's voice sounded husky, although his bronchitis had cleared up now. He shook hands with Luke and kissed Mum on both cheeks. "Goodbye,

Elizabeth, and thank you. Take care of that fine boy, now."

"And you take care of yourself," said Mum. Her voice sounded strange, too. She took Luke's hand and hurried him away, through the doors and outside, bundling him up into the front seat of the van.

Luke tried to see through the glass doors if Mr Bronzovi and Bushy were waving to him, but suddenly his eyes were watery and blurred.

* * * * *

It was hard work getting settled into the new house, but it was fun, too. At first everything was a muddle, with boxes standing about and nothing in its place. But slowly things got straighter.

Mum put up curtains and laid rugs on the bare floorboards.

Luke piled all his books and toys in a heap beside the bed in his new room, while Hammy whizzed round on his wheel.

"What we need is shelves for storing things," said Mum. "I wish I'd learnt a bit of carpentry some time or other. I'm hopeless at things like that."

It was true that Mum was much better at gardening and outdoor things than jobs about the house. They usually ended up leaving things in piles and going to pick raspberries, or to weed the new little lettuces.

Luke picked a big bunch of pink roses

and Mum put them into a blue jug. It was beginning to look like home.

* * * * *

Every day Luke remembered to look across the park to see if Mr Bronzovi and Bushy were coming across to visit. He stared hard until his eyes watered, but he could not pick them out from other people and dogs. He had almost forgotten whereabouts in the apartment block their own home had been.

"I think it's too far for them to walk across," said Mum. "Maybe Mr Bronzovi will come on the bus one day."

"I don't think Bushy would like the bus," said Luke.

The traffic sounds were quieter here, muffled and far away. But the nights were full of mysterious new noises. There was an owl that hooted in the tree at the edge of the back garden. The pear tree brushed its leaves against Luke's window whenever there was a breeze. At dusk, bats darted through the air and swooped about their heads. Luke could hear their tiny squeaky voices, which were too high for Mum's ears.

* * * * *

One night, Luke thought he heard a different noise. A whimpering sound, and a noise of something scratching. He had been asleep and thought he might still be dreaming. But when he rolled over and sat up in bed it was still there.

"Mum!" called Luke. Mum didn't answer. She was sound asleep in her own room, tired out from a day of clearing weeds and brambles from the back garden. Luke got out of bed and padded to the door.

He would have to wake her, because he was sure there was something strange outside. He felt a little bit scared.

Then the noise came again, and he knew what it was. A dog! A dog, whimpering and whining, scrabbling at the front door. His heart began to thump. He switched on the light and ran downstairs.

"Who's there?" he said to the inside of the closed door.

He was answered by a joyful yelp. He ran to the door and unlocked it, pulling it open and letting in the soft night air. And then Bushy came in too, bounding forward and almost knocking him off his feet.

10

All Together Again

Mum came running downstairs, pulling on her dressing-gown. Bushy danced around both of them, tongue hanging out and tail waving. Luke danced around too, until Mum said they were making her feel dizzy. She also looked rather puzzled.

"Whatever is he doing here? It's three o'clock in the morning!"

"He found us!" said Luke. "Isn't he clever? He found our new house, all by himself!"

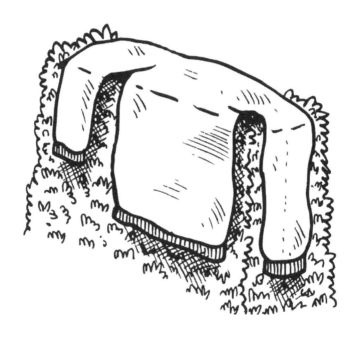

"So it seems," said Mum. "I suppose he wanders all over the park at night. He probably smelled our smell around the garden – you left your sweatshirt out by the hedge and your trainers on the steps. I wish he'd waited for daylight before waking us up though."

Luke hooked his fingers through Bushy's collar. He looked pleadingly at Mum. "He didn't know. Please, Mum, could he stay? Just until morning? Just this once?"

Mum looked very doubtful. Luke thought she was going to say no, and bundle Bushy outside again. But she said, "Well, just this once. But it's not to become a habit. I need my sleep."

She gave a huge yawn and closed and fastened the door.

Mum was still half-asleep, or she would never have let Luke take Bushy to his bedroom. But she yawned again, and went upstairs, and didn't seem to notice. Luke got into bed and tried to make Bushy settle down on the rug beside the bed. He thought it would be very nice to lie in bed and reach out a hand to feel Bushy's rough, warm coat in the darkness.

But Bushy wouldn't settle. He lay for a few moments, to oblige, then got up and prowled around the room. He whined and scratched at the door.

Luke thought perhaps he was hungry or thirsty. He got out of bed and took Bushy down to the kitchen. But Bushy didn't want the water or the sausage meat that Luke offered him. He ran to the front door and scrabbled at it.

"Oh, Bushy," said Luke. "I thought you'd want to stay with me."

Bushy came and licked his hand apologetically. But he went straight back to the door again, turning to look pleadingly at Luke. It was beginning to get light outside.

Upstairs, Mum's door suddenly flew open and Mum came downstairs, fully dressed. Luke felt that he and Bushy were in for a telling-off.

"Sorry, Mum," he said quickly. "We didn't mean to make a noise."

Mum was frowning. "It's all right, Luke. I suddenly had an awful thought. Something might be wrong with Mr Bronzovi, and Bushy tried to tell us. I think we'd better find out. I've tried to phone but there's no answer. Go and get dressed, and we'll catch the early bus."

Bushy seemed happier now that they

were getting ready to go out. But he refused food and drink and sat waiting by the door all the time they were making tea and toast and waiting for the bus.

Bushy shot off across the park as soon as the door was opened. By the time the bus reached their old block, he was there by the crossing, panting, waiting for them.

Mum let herself into Mr Bronzovi's apartment with the key she'd had when he had been ill. Bushy bounded ahead, but Mum told Luke to wait just inside the hall door. He waited, holding his breath, his heart racing. It was quiet in the apartment, not a sound. Mum went into the bedroom and Bushy went in too.

Then Mum called out, and Luke let

out his breath. "It's all right, Luke. He's not well again, but you can come in, if you're quiet."

Mr Bronzovi was in bed, very still and small-looking under the covers. His cheeks were hollow because his teeth were out, and there was a bluish look around his mouth. But his eyes were the same.

"Bit of a bad turn," said Mum. "I'm calling the ambulance."

While she phoned, Luke stayed with Mr Bronzovi. He said, "Bushy came to fetch us. Mum guessed you might be ill again."

"Ah!" said Mr Bronzovi. "What a dog that is! He knew, last night, that something was wrong. He is one in a million."

His voice sounded very weak, but Luke felt much better for hearing it. He could see Bushy felt better too, sitting looking at them with his head cocked.

One of the paramedics said that Mr Bronzovi had had a slight heart attack. She said that he must go into hospital for a day or two, for tests. Then he should consider going into a home for elderly people, where he could be looked after. He would get better, with rest and medicine, but he did need proper food and proper care. Luke sat very quietly and held Bushy's collar while the paramedics took Mr Bronzovi away.

Afterwards, the cluttered apartment seemed very empty. Bushy flopped down with his head on his paws, watching Luke. Luke wanted to cry, but Mum kept finding things for him to do, so there was no time. There were things he wanted to ask, but Mum was bustling round tidying and sorting out. She said she would be going to the hospital later, with clean pyjamas and other things for Mr Bronzovi.

"What will happen to Bushy?" asked Luke in a small voice.

Mum came and sat down opposite, clutching a pile of towels. She said, "I've been thinking. Luke, Mr Bronzovi can't look after himself any more. How would you like it if he came and lived with us? I'm sure it could be arranged. We've got the room. He'd enjoy the garden, and pottering around. And we'd enjoy having him, wouldn't we?"

Luke jumped up and joyfully punched the air. "Yes!" he shouted. Then he said, "What about Bushy, though? Could he come too?"

"I've thought about that, too. I don't see why not. There are no rules about not having dogs there. I'd quite like a dog about. And I know you'd like it."

"Yes!" shouted Luke again, and Bushy thumped his tail.

* * * * *

In less than a week, Mr Bronzovi and Bushy had moved in. It felt to Luke as though they had always been there. Mr Bronzovi was feeling much better and looked almost as well as ever. Mum liked his company, and was glad of him to be there with Luke when she went back to work.

"And I'll get those shelves up, soon as I'm properly on my feet," promised Mr Bronzovi. "I've always loved a bit of carpentry."

* * * * *

Bushy settled into the house and garden and felt at home in no time at all. He proved it by burying a bone under the raspberry bushes. "That means it's his territory now," said Mr Bronzovi, sitting in a garden chair in the shade. "I don't think he'll ever go back to that place in the park any more."

"Everything's worked out just right, hasn't it, Mr Bronzovi?" said Luke. "For all of us. Now we'll all live happy ever after, won't we?"

Mr Bronzovi thought for a moment. Then he said, "We'll live happy ever after all right. One day, when we've lived our lives here and go to live with God in heaven. That'll be wonderful. But we won't be going just yet. There's the rest of our lives here first, and I dare say it won't all be easy. But we've got God to help us."

"He answered a lot of prayers for us, didn't he?" said Luke.

"He did," agreed Mr Bronzovi. "Not always in the way we thought we wanted. But always the right thing in the end, even in the hard things."

"Will more hard things happen?" asked Luke. The sky was so blue, the sun so warm, and everything had worked out so well that he couldn't believe they ever would.

"Oh, there'll be more," said Mr Bronzovi. "But we'll get through, with God's help. Learning to trust him, a bit more each time."

Luke thought about this, sitting on the grass and looking at Bushy, who had already forgotten where he had buried the bone and was sniffing around for the place.

"Like Bushy learnt to trust us," he said. "A bit more each time. When he was nobody's dog."

"Tak," said Mr Bronzovi.

Discussion Questions

1. Luke liked his third-floor apartment because he could look out over the road and the park. What do you like about your home?

2. Why did Luke think the stray dog didn't have a home? Imagine you are a stray dog. How would you feel?

3. Why did Luke name the dog Bushy? There are two reasons!

4. Luke wondered why God had let Bushy be hurt. What did Mr Bronzovi say that they must do? What things make you sad and angry? Do you think Mr Bronzovi's advice would help you?

5. Why didn't Bushy trust anyone in the beginning?

6. At first, Luke's mum didn't want him to get involved with the stray dog. Do you think she was sensible?

7. Mr Bronzovi says God cares about animals, so he and Luke pray about Bushy. What does prayer mean? Is there anything you would like to pray about?

8. How did Luke feel when Bushy was taken away? Have you ever had something or someone precious taken away from you?

9. According to Mr Bronzovi, who worked out all the problems for the best? What do you think about this? Do you agree?

10. What did you like most about this story? Did you learn anything that could help you with your life?

If you have any questions you would like to ask the author, please ask your parents' or carers' permission, and use the contact form on the Dernier Publishing website:

www.dernierpublishing.com

If you enjoyed this book you may also like to read:

The Birthday Shoes
by Mary Weeks Millard

Emily Jane hates her new shoes, until they take her on exciting adventures. . .

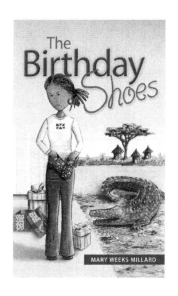

"It made me feel like I was there." – Susanna

I Want to Be an Airline Pilot
by Mary Weeks Millard

Shema has no parents, but he discovers through a series of exciting adventures that he has a Father in heaven.

"I really enjoyed this book, it is one of my favourites." - Kemi